THE LITTLE
TIN SOLDIER

Once there was a one-legged little tin soldier who lived in a little boy's cupboard with lots of other toys.

One day, he got left on a window ledge. A strong wind came by and blew him out of the window!

Two young boys found the little soldier on the pavement. They made him a little paper boat and sent him sailing down a nearby stream.

The little soldier sailed his boat all the
way to the ocean. But then a big fish
swallowed him up!

Luckily, a fisherman caught that fish and sold it at the market. Guess who bought it? The little boy's mother!

When she opened the fish up, she found the little toy soldier and gave it back to her overjoyed son.

That night, safely back in his toy cupboard, the soldier told his toy friends, "It was fun to see the world in a boat of my own, but all in all, there's no place like home!"

THE UGLY DUCKLING

One day a mama duck hatched a lot of little baby ducks.

But one was gray, and different from all the other yellow ducklings.

"Oh, you're ugly!" they all quacked.

The poor little ugly duckling looked at himself in the lily pond. He didn't look like a little duck at all.

"What's wrong with me?" he asked
a frog near the garden wall. "Why are
my feet so big and my neck so long?"

Then he asked a little swan,
"Why don't I fit in at all?"

"That's because you're a beautiful swan like me!" she said. "You're not an ugly duckling after all!"